PUFFIN BOOKS

Dancing Shoes

MAKING THE GRADE

Antonia Barber was born in London and grew up in Sussex. While studying English at London University, she spent her evenings at the Royal Opera House, where her father worked, watching the ballet and meeting many famous dancers. She married a fellow student and lived in New York before settling back in England. She has three children, including a daughter who did ballet from the age of three and attended the Royal Ballet School Junior Classes at Sadler's Wells.

Her best-known books are *The Ghosts*, which was runner-up for the Carnegie Medal and was filmed as *The Amazing Mr Blunden*, and *The Mousehole Cat*. She has also written *Tales from the Ballet*.

Antonia lives in an old oast house in Kent and a little fisherman's cottage in Cornwall.

D0313077

If you like dancing and making friends, you'll love

DANCING SHOES

Lucy Lambert – Lou to her friends – dreams of one day becoming a great ballerina. Find out if Lucy's dream comes true in:

DANCING SHOES: LESSONS FOR LUCY
DANCING SHOES: INTO THE SPOTLIGHT
DANCING SHOES: FRIENDS AND RIVALS
DANCING SHOES: OUT OF STEP
DANCING SHOES: LUCY'S NEXT STEP

And look out for more DANCING SHOES titles coming soon

Antonia Barber

DANCING SHOES
Making the Grade

Illustrated by Biz Hull

PUFFIN BOOKS

PUFFIN BOOKS

Published by the Penguin Group
Penguin Books Ltd, 27 Wrights Lane, London W8 5TZ, England
Penguin Putnam Inc., 375 Hudson Street, New York, New York 10014, USA
Penguin Books Australia Ltd, Ringwood, Victoria, Australia
Penguin Books Canada Ltd, 10 Alcorn Avenue, Toronto, Ontario, Canada M4V 3B2
Penguin Books (NZ) Ltd, Private Bag 102902, NSMC, Auckland, New Zealand

Penguin Books Ltd, Registered Offices: Harmondsworth, Middlesex, England

First published 1999
3

Text copyright © Antonia Barber, 1999
Illustrations copyright © Biz Hull, 1999
All rights reserved

The moral right of the author and illustrator has been asserted

Typeset in 15/22 Monotype Calisto

Made and printed in England by Clays Ltd, St Ives plc

British Library Cataloguing in Publication Data
A CIP catalogue record for this book is available from the British Library

ISBN 0-141-30149-X

Chapter One

Lucy Lambert yawned, stretched, opened
her eyes and reached for her new
scrapbook. She turned
to the first page
to admire a rather

unflattering picture of herself with red eyes clutching a silver cup.

Her bedroom door flew open and her best friend, Emma Browne, flumped on to the end of her bed.

'Can I share your bathroom?' she said. 'Ours is full of boys.'

Emma's parents owned the house where both girls lived. Lucy's family rented the basement flat, but most of the time the two girls felt as if they lived together.

'How many are there?' asked Lou with interest.

'Only Martin and his friend, but it feels like half a dozen.'

Lou hardly knew Emma's brother. Martin was fourteen and went away to boarding school. Now he had a friend staying with him for the Easter holiday.

'What are they doing today?'

'Chamber of Horrors and the London Dungeon.'

'Again? I don't suppose we can go too?'

Emma shook her head. The boys didn't like to be seen out with the younger girls. It was bad for their street cred.

Lou couldn't see the point of having a brother who was never there. She thought her own little brother, Charlie, was much nicer.

'Let's see your scrapbook.' Emma took it out of her hands and read aloud the headline above the picture. '*INJURED DANCER TAKES THE PRIZE*. It's not a very good picture,' she said.

'I was blinking,' said Lou. 'It was the flash.'

Emma read on: '*Young Lucy Lambard* . . . they spelt your name wrong . . . *was heartbroken when an injured ankle . . .'*

'It was my knee,' said Lou.

*'. . . stopped her from dancing in the Maple
School of Ballet's Annual Competition. But
her tears turned to joy . . .'*

'Ugh!' said Lou.

*'. . . when the judges, ex-Bolshoi dancer
Irina Barashkova and ballet school principal
Miss Penelope Maple awarded her the Maple
Cup for Progress. Miss Maple told an audience
of parents and friends that late-starter Lucy*

had worked very hard and showed exceptional talent. Blinking back tears . . .'

'Enough!' shouted Lou, but Emma went on, *'Lucy told our reporter, "I want to be a famous ballerina and dance in* Romeo and Juliet *at the Opera House."'*

Lucy cringed. 'I didn't even say that!' she protested. 'I just said "yes" when the reporter asked me if I'd like to be a ballet dancer, and *"Romeo and Juliet"* when he asked me my favourite ballet.'

Jem had teased her mercilessly about that bit. 'I want to be a famous ballerina!' he would cry, sniffing hard and fluttering his eyelashes. Jem Sinclair was the only boy in their ballet class and Lucy thought perhaps he was just a little bit jealous. After all, he had won the class prize and only got his name in the list at the bottom of the page.

'It's pretty awful, isn't it?' she said.

'Well, yes,' said Emma honestly, 'but it *is* your very first newspaper cutting, so it's sort of special. I mean, one day this scrapbook will be full of them . . .'

'And I'll be tall and graceful,' said Lou dreamily, 'wearing a white embroidered tutu . . .'

'. . . with your arms full of flowers,' added Emma.

They both sighed.

'Martin goes back to school at the weekend,' said Emma.

'And Jem comes home from Scotland tomorrow,' added Lou.

He had gone to stay with some cousins while his grandparents, who looked after him, were working in America.

'So does Angela,' said Emma, '. . . from France somewhere.'

'Oh, *Angela*,' said Lou crossly. 'For all I care she can stay there!'

'She's not *that* bad,' said Emma. 'I think . . .'

'She's a mean bully,' interrupted Lou. 'Just because she's not bullying *you* any more, you think she's nice now. But she's still being horrible to me!'

'It's because she doesn't know you,' said Emma. 'I mean, you don't go to our school . . . you only see her once a week at ballet class.'

'And that's once too often,' growled Lou.

There was a long silence. It was getting close to a quarrel and they both looked for a way out.

'Well, at least your granny went back to Worthing,' said Lou, changing the subject.

Granny Browne was very bossy. She was always making people do things they didn't want to do.

'But only because Martin needed his room,' said Emma gloomily. 'She's coming back once he's gone.'

'What's her excuse this time?'

'Her flat's being painted and she says the smell of paint makes her ill.'

They both groaned. They didn't trust Granny Browne. They knew that she really wanted to live in the Lamberts' flat.

'Promise me you'll never move out,' said Emma anxiously.

'Of course not!' said Lou.

'Even if your mum passes her exams and gets a brilliant job?'

'Not even then,' said Lou.

After all, Emma was her *best* friend.

Chapter Two

A week later they were back in the noisy changing room of the Maple School of Ballet. Lou and Emma were welcomed with smiles and hugs by the young ones in the Beginners' Class. Angela's friends said hello to Emma but went out of their way to ignore Lou.

Angela seemed strangely quiet. Lou wondered if losing the class prize to Jem had made her a little less sure of herself.

'I'll do your hair first,' Lou said,

gathering Emma's straight fair hair into a bun.

Some of the side bits fell out and Emma moaned.

'I told my mum she was cutting it too short!'

'It'll soon grow,' said Lou comfortingly and stuck in a few extra pins.

While Emma was dealing with her own long hair, Lou glanced

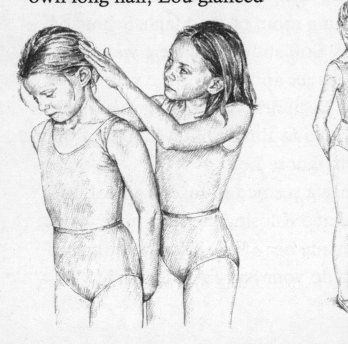

sideways at Angela. She looked thinner
. . . as if she hadn't been well. Maybe she
had caught one of those bugs while she
was away on holiday.

When Emma had finished, they rushed
off to the studio to see Jem before class
began.

'How was Scotland?' asked Lou.

'Pretty good . . . very healthy!'

They could see that just by looking at
him.

'What are your cousins like?'

'A bit posh . . .'

Before they could ask him any more,
Mrs Dennison came in and the class took
their places.

After the *révérence* they had a gentle
warming-up session. Most of them were
out of practice after the Easter holiday,
but Lou and Emma had been lucky. Mrs

Dillon, who lived in the flat on the top floor of the Brownes' house, was really Irina Barashkova. She had once been a ballet dancer with the Russian Bolshoi Company and she had given the two girls some holiday practice sessions.

Lou felt marvellous as she did her *demipliés, tendues* and *glissées*. Even her *pas de chat*, the little cat-leap, now flowed smoothly from side to side. The piece in the newspaper, about having 'exceptional talent', had given her a confidence she hadn't felt before. She had always compared herself to Angela, who had been doing ballet for years. Now she felt she could do anything she set her heart on . . . and Angela's famously long legs suddenly looked a bit skinny.

Mrs Dennison finished the lesson early to give them all a pep talk. They were taking their grade exam at the end of the term and she told them that they must work very hard.

'You each have strengths on which you must build,' she said, 'and weaknesses that you must overcome if you are to get good grades.'

She spoke to each of them in turn, beginning with Emma and praising her for listening carefully and remembering what she was taught. 'But you must be more confident,' she went on. 'You are a better dancer than you think, Emma, and you must learn to "show off" a little when you dance.'

Emma turned pink at the very thought.

To Jem Mrs Dennison said, 'You have great energy and flair, which are important in a male dancer. But at times this makes you headstrong. Remember that energy is wasted unless it is properly controlled.'

When she came to Angela she told her that she danced well and with a natural grace. 'But you must try to connect with your audience,' she said. 'Never forget that you are dancing for them.'

Lou felt her heart beat faster when it was her turn.

'Now Lucy is a dancer who loves her audience,' said Mrs Dennison.

It was true, thought Lou, and wondered if that was good or bad . . . Did it mean that she was just a show-off?

Mrs Dennison saw her anxious face and smiled. 'This is your strong point,' she told Lou. 'Your dancing gives you pleasure and you share that with your audience. Your problem is that you lack concentration; your mind is always wandering when you are in class.'

Lou nodded. She knew it was true.

'Go home now,' Mrs Dennison told them, 'and think about what I have said. Build on your strengths, overcome your weaknesses and you will all do well in your grade exams.'

'Old Dennison is all right,' said Jem as they walked home. 'I mean, she tells it like it is . . . she doesn't treat us like kids.'

'She's a bit scary,' said Emma. 'She's so strict.'

'Yes, but she's a good teacher,' said Lou, 'and that's what matters. It's no use having a teacher who's fun if you don't learn anything. I mean, it's what teachers are for.'

'Well, she's got you sussed,' said Jem. 'I see you in class, lost in a dream in the middle of your *pliés*.'

'She's got you sussed too!' said Lou. 'You like dancing, but you don't like it when she makes you put your foot at the right angle! Ballet isn't just leaping about, you know.'

Jem looked annoyed. 'Yes, well, I don't really want to do ballet. I'm only doing it to get into stage school,' he said. 'Prancing about in tights and embroidered jackets is not my scene! I want to do something more exciting.'

This was a blow: Lou had set her heart on having Jem for her partner when she became a famous ballerina.

'But ballet *is* exciting!' she said indignantly.

'All those princes and airy fairies,' he mocked.

Lou thought quickly. 'What about the sword fight in *Romeo and Juliet*? That's pretty exciting!'

Jem shrugged. 'I've never seen *Romeo and Juliet*,' he said.

Lou decided that it was high time he did.

Chapter Three

Something was wrong in the Brownes' part
of the house. Granny Browne was back
now that Martin had returned to his
boarding school, and there were raised
voices which reached Lou in the basement.

'I'm going up to see if Emma's all
right,' Lou told her mother, who was
busy revising for her exams. 'You know
she hates quarrels.'

Jenny Lambert put down her books
and gave her a shrewd look. 'Hmm!' she

said. 'Well, you can go up to Emma's room . . . but no listening at keyholes!'

'Would I?' said Lou.

'Like a shot,' said her mother, who knew her well.

Emma wasn't in her room. She was sitting on the stairs listening with wide eyes to the loud voices which came from the kitchen.

Lou sat beside her. 'What is it?' she asked.

'Something awful.' Emma's face was pinched and white.

'But what?'

'I think . . . I think my dad has lost his job!'

Lou thought she must have heard wrong. 'Your dad?' she said. 'But he's ever so important . . . at the bank, I mean . . . How could he lose his job?'

'I don't know,' said Emma. 'Something about his bank being overtaken by a bigger bank.'

They sat in silence, straining their ears.

Lou couldn't believe it. She really liked Mr Browne. He had refitted the basement kitchen for her mum and now he was doing the same for Mrs Dillon upstairs. What would happen if he had lost his job? Would he have to sell the house?

'You won't have to move away, will you?' she asked.

Emma looked miserable. 'I don't know,' she said.

There was a terrible sick feeling in the pit of Lou's stomach. She remembered all the troubles they had had before the Brownes bought the house – how the old landlord had tried to get them out of their flat. If Mr Browne had lost his job, she might lose her home as well as her best friend. She put an arm around Emma's shoulder and hugged her.

The kitchen door opened. In a flash they were up the stairs and out of sight.

'I'm not discussing it any more.' It was Mr Browne's voice. 'I'm going to work in the shed.'

They heard him go out through the back door.

'He always goes out to the shed when he's upset,' said Emma.

Mr Browne loved his tools and his carpentry; he liked them better than banking.

He had left the kitchen door ajar. They crept back down the stairs.

Granny Browne's voice came loud and clear. 'He'll never find another job with all these takeovers.'

'It's his decision.' Mrs Browne's voice was weary but calm.

'After all that expensive education I gave him!'

Granny Browne sounded as if she might explode. Lou wished she would . . . in a puff of smoke . . . with just a little heap of ashes left on the Brownes' kitchen floor.

The voice whined on. 'He'll have to sell this house!'

'He's trying to work it all out, Ethel.'
Mrs Browne seemed really fed up.

'Ethel!' hissed Lou. 'Is her name Ethel?'

Emma nodded and they both giggled
nervously.

'How will he pay the children's school
fees?' Granny Browne's voice grew shrill.
'Or are you going to shove them into some
awful local school?'

Lou and Jem went to the local school
and it wasn't awful at all, it was very good.
Lou felt like rushing in and telling her so.

'Perhaps I can come to your school
now,' whispered Emma hopefully. 'If they
can't pay my fees, I mean.' She had always
wanted to go to school with her two
friends.

'That would be great!' said Lou. But it
would be no use, she thought, if the
Brownes had to move away.

They heard Mrs Browne's voice: 'I have to go downstairs and have a word with Jenny . . .' She had clearly had enough of Granny Browne's moaning.

The girls dashed upstairs again. 'They'll be drinking coffee and nattering for the next hour,' said Lou. 'Let's go up and see Mrs Dillon.'

Mrs Dillon was a good comforter. As she made them hot chocolate, they admired her new kitchen. Then they sat on the sofa and told her about all their worries.

'Pouff!' said the old lady. 'This is being a storm in a cup. Perhaps you are getting the stick the wrong way round.'

'I don't think so,' said Emma. 'Granny Browne was in a real temper!'

Mrs Dillon snorted. 'She is silly old woman.'

There was a knock at the door and Mr Browne came in carrying two long, heavy boxes.

'Ah! It is my window boxes!' Mrs Dillon seemed very pleased. 'For the first time since I am a girl,' she told Lou and Emma, 'I am having my own little garden!'

The girls watched with interest as Mr Browne fixed the boxes behind the parapet outside the attic windows.

'You're a brilliant carpenter,' said Lou admiringly. 'Why didn't you do that instead of boring old banking?'

Mr Browne looked at her thoughtfully. 'You think I should have been a carpenter?' he said.

'Yes, I do,' said Lou. 'I mean, it makes you happy and it makes other people happy too . . . with new kitchens and windows boxes and things.'

'Well,' said Mr Browne, 'out of the mouths of babes . . .' He smiled at her and went off downstairs again.

'What did he mean . . . about babes?' Lou asked Mrs Dillon.

'It is old proverb,' she said. 'It means that children are often having more sense than grown-ups.'

'Oh well,' said Lou, 'everyone knows *that*!'

Chapter Four

They were practising their *battements*, little taps on the floor with pointed toes. They were in Emma's room, where Mr Browne had fixed up a *barre* in front of a big old mirror. Lou had turned on the baby monitor so that they could hear if Charlie woke up in the flat downstairs. Jenny had gone to her evening class.

Mrs Dillon raised Emma's chin a little and turned out Jem's foot. Then she said, 'Begin.'

(Battements tendus, *starting in first position* . . .) Lou thought about *Romeo and Juliet*. Jenny had found the video at the local library and they were going to watch it after their practice (. . . *and down into* demi-plié *and stretch* . . .). She felt sure that Jem would change his mind when he saw the fight scene. He couldn't say that was 'airy fairy' (. . . *and three times in front, closing into first position*). It made her really miserable to think that he might not love ballet the way she did.

'Lucy!' said Mrs Dillon sternly. 'What did Mrs Dennison tell you about keeping your mind on your dancing?'

Lou bit her lip. I *must* concentrate, she told herself severely.

Next it was *battements glissés*, with the foot just brushing the floor (*First position, hands on* barre *and* . . .). What did Jem

mean when he said he wanted to do something more exciting? (. . . glissé *into second position and closing into first*). Once he had told her he might decide to be a footballer, which would be a terrible waste . . . Oh, no! She was doing it again. She shut out every thought of Jem and tried to make sure that the arch and angle of her foot were just right.

When the practice was over, they went down to Lou's flat, where the video was already set up. She fetched orange juice and biscuits and made Mrs Dillon a cup of tea. Then they all settled down to watch *Romeo and Juliet*.

The opening shot with the red and gold curtains of the Opera House reminded Lou of the evening when Mrs Dillon had made her watch her first ballet. Before that, she had never thought of being a dancer, but *Romeo and Juliet* had changed her life. If only Jem could feel a little of the same thrill, he would have to admit that ballet was better than stupid football.

The red curtains parted to reveal a crowded town square full of colour and movement. The music filled Lou's head and she longed to be dancing instead of watching. She glanced sideways to see if Jem was enjoying it. He seemed to like the action bits, especially when the sword fight broke out between the two groups of young men.

'I know this bit,' he said.

'You said you hadn't seen it before.'

'Well, not quite like this.' He wouldn't explain.

The two lovers were danced by Rudolf Nureyev and Margot Fonteyn. Lou's heart leaped as Juliet made her first entrance at the ball. In a simple white dress, she came shyly and gracefully down a grand flight of steps. One day, thought Lou, I'll make an entrance just like that.

The ballet was exciting and beautiful,

but it did not have a happy ending. Everyone died and Lou and Emma sniffed and snuffled.

Jem sighed. 'Could you two please turn off the waterworks,' he said, 'before the basement gets flooded!'

Then Charlie woke up and came out, trailing his teddy bear. Lou and Emma knew that if he saw them both crying, he was likely to join in, so they put on cheerful smiles as he climbed on to Jem's lap. He liked Jem, who sometimes kicked a football around with him in the back garden. But before Charlie could settle down, Jenny arrived home and he found himself heading back to his cot.

Lou and Emma went up on to the steps to see Jem off. As he unlocked his bike chain, Lou said, 'Well?'

'Well, what?' He grinned at her.

'What did you think of the ballet? I
mean, you can't say that wasn't exciting.'

'It *was* pretty good,' he admitted, 'but
if you come round to our place one
evening, I'll show you a different version
of *Romeo and Juliet*.'

'Who's in it?' Lou demanded. She

33

didn't see how anyone could be better than Margot Fonteyn and Rudolf Nureyev.

'Wait and see,' he said annoyingly. 'You come too, Em, and I'll show you both the sort of ballet *I* want to do.'

Chapter Five

As Lou and Emma strapped Charlie into his push-chair, Jenny said, 'How would you like a trip to the Cosy Corner this morning?'

'Oh, great!' said Lou.

'My favourite!' said Emma.

The Cosy Corner was a tea-room with wonderful home-made cakes, but it was rather expensive.

'Is it a special treat?' asked Lou.

'Well, sort of . . . Mr Mumford has

invited you both.'

Lou thought about it as she helped
Jenny to bump the push-chair up the
basement steps. Mr Mumford was
Angela's grandfather. Lou and Emma
called him the Wind-up Merchant
because he teased them a lot. Lou could
never understand how someone so
nice could have a granddaughter
who was a mean bully.

'Will Angela be there?' she asked, frowning.

'Well, yes,' said Jenny. 'That's what it's all about. He's worried because she's not eating well.'

They reached the top of the steps and set out for the street market.

'She does look a bit thinner this term,' said Emma.

'Her legs look quite skinny,' said Lou.

'It seems it started while they were in France,' said her mother. 'Angela complained that she didn't like the French food. They thought she would be better when they got home, but Mr Mumford says that she has quite lost her appetite.'

'And does she like cream cakes?' asked Emma.

'Well, I don't know . . .' Lou's mother

sounded a bit doubtful. 'Her grandfather thinks the sight of you lot stuffing yourselves will encourage her to eat.'

Lou hooted. 'More likely put her off for life!'

'That's what I thought,' said Jenny, 'but I didn't like to say so.'

'Why didn't the Wind-up Merchant ask us himself?' Lou thought it was all a bit odd.

'He wants Angela to think it's a spur-of-the moment thing . . . not a plot to make her eat.'

The lights changed and they went over the crossing.

'We're meeting Jem in the market,' said Lou.

'Oh, I think he's invited too,' said Jenny.

*

They were sorting through a pile of old comics on the second-hand bookstall when the Wind-up Merchant arrived. Angela trailed behind him, looking as snooty as ever. He greeted them warmly and said, 'Why don't we all have a cake and a glass of lemonade?' as if he had just thought of it.

Lou said, 'Oh, great!' and Jem said, 'Good idea!' as if they hadn't been expecting it.

Emma went slightly pink. She was hopeless, thought Lou, when it came to any sort of pretence.

They crowded into the tea-shop, which smelt deliciously of vanilla and ground coffee, and settled themselves round a big table in the far corner.

The Cosy Corner made the best meringues in the world, but they tended

to explode when you bit into them. Lou
was not planning to spend her time
wiping cream off the end of her nose . . .
not with Angela watching, so she chose a
big juicy-looking strawberry tart. Jem and
Emma chose meringues. Angela said she
wasn't hungry.

'Nonsense! Nonsense!' said the Wind-
up Merchant cheerfully and ordered her a
strawberry tart like Lou's.

He knew his granddaughter well
enough to know that she would not be
caught dead eating an exploding
meringue. He asked them what they had
been doing in the holidays and Jem told
them all about Scotland. Lou was quite
put out to find that his cousin Ellie could
row a boat and had taken Jem picnicking
on an island.

'Does she do ballet?' she demanded.

Jem laughed. 'She's mad about boats and having adventures,' he told her. 'A bit like someone out of *Swallows and Amazons*. And no! She doesn't do ballet!'

The strawberry tart was mouth-watering but Angela just picked at hers. She fished out the strawberries with her fork but left the pastry and the cream.

'Eat up,' said her grandfather. 'Look at Lou, she's made short work of hers!'

Angela looked at Lou and then at Lou's empty plate, and her lip curled.

'Would you like another one?' the Wind-up Merchant asked Lou hopefully.

Lou would have *loved* another one, but she couldn't face Angela's sneers.

'It was lovely, thanks,' she said with a sigh, 'but I think I'm full up.'

Jem said 'yes' eagerly to a second meringue, but Emma was still wrestling with the first one. I should have warned her that they explode, thought Lou.

A voice, raised in anger, reached them from outside, muffled by the clinking of cups and forks. Looking up, they saw Granny Browne beyond the window, waving her sharp little finger at one of the stallholders. Lou felt like ducking under the table.

Emma's face clouded as if the day had

suddenly grown cold.

'Are you all right, Emma?' asked the Wind-up Merchant.

She looked at him miserably. There was something about his round, good-humoured face that made him easy to confide in. Suddenly Emma found herself telling him how her dad had lost his job and how awful Granny Browne was being.

'She says we'll have to sell the house and Dad won't be able to afford our school fees . . . Well, I wouldn't mind that if I could go to school with Lou and Jem, but if we had to move away . . .'

He listened to her with quiet attention, as if she had been a grown-up.

When she had finished, Lou said, 'I think Emma's dad should be a carpenter instead of working in a bank. I mean, it's

43

what he likes doing and he's really good at it.'

'Only Granny Browne thinks carpenters are not important enough,' Emma explained.

Lou told him all about the new kitchens Mr Browne had fitted for her mother and Mrs Dillon, '. . . and he made her some brilliant window boxes!'

'She's going to plant herbs,' said Emma. 'She likes them better than flowers.'

Lou had a sudden thought. 'I don't suppose you need a new kitchen, do you?' she asked the Wind-up Merchant.

He looked very solemn and said that funnily enough, Angela's mother, who ran the house for him, had been complaining about the kitchen only the other day.

'Then you'd better have a word with Emma's dad,' said Lou eagerly. 'He'll soon fix it for you!'

The Wind-up Merchant said he might just do that.

Chapter Six

'Who's in this ballet then?' asked Lou.

'Wait and see,' said Jem. 'And it's not exactly a ballet.'

'But you said . . .'

'I said it was another version of *Romeo and Juliet.*'

'You said it was the sort of ballet you wanted to do.'

'Well, it is a sort of ballet.'

Jem was fiddling with the video, fast-forwarding to find the part he wanted.

They were all round at Jem's house
and they had just finished one of Jem's
grandmother's wonderful West Indian
meals. Orly Sinclair was a really good
cook, as well as being a famous singer.

'Why don't you just start the tape at the
beginning,' said Lou impatiently.

'I have my reasons,' said Jem, 'and
anyway it's ready now.'

He flopped back on to the long sofa
and pushed his way between Lou and

Emma. Angela, who was sitting on the other side of Emma, looked a bit miffed because he hadn't chosen to sit next to her.

Lou couldn't see why Orly had invited Angela. Why were the grown-ups always trying to make them be friends? It's not my fault if we're not, she thought. I can't help it if Angela hates me. She's always so stuck-up . . . She had even been sniffy about Orly's meal, picking listlessly at the food while the others tucked in.

Orly came from the kitchen and settled herself in a comfy chair. 'Let's get this show on the road,' she said, and Jem pressed the button.

Somehow, Lou had expected red velvet curtains like the opening of *Romeo and Juliet*. Instead, she saw a bleak landscape of city streets, through which moved the distant but threatening figures of a gang of teenage boys.

'You've got the wrong video,' she said.

'Pipe down and watch it,' said Jem.

The camera moved in closer, showing the boys, hard-faced and tough, as they stalked like jungle animals through the crumbling streets.

'But it's not ballet,' protested Lou, 'and it's not *Romeo and Juliet!*'

Jem ignored her.

The gang of boys met up with another gang; each group mocked and insulted the other. They weren't really dancing at first, but every now and then, they would break into sharp, patterned steps that sent a shiver up Lou's spine. Then a fight broke out and she saw how each movement was planned and skilfully danced. Against her will, she found herself drawn into the story unfolding on the screen.

But it was not until the girl appeared that Lou realized that it really was *Romeo and Juliet*. Shy but excited at her first dance, she walked into the hall in her simple white dress, just like Margot Fonteyn in the ballet. But her name was Maria and the boy she loved was called Tony.

'What is this?' Lou demanded. 'I mean, it's sort of the same, only it's different.'

Orly smiled. 'It's *West Side Story*,' she said. 'It's a musical based on *Romeo and Juliet* but set in modern New York.'

'Can you do that?' asked Emma. 'I mean, just take a story from a ballet and use it for something else?' She felt that this was stealing and Lou agreed with her.

'But the ballet was taken from one of Shakespeare's plays,' Jem pointed out.

'And Shakespeare took it from an earlier story,' added Orly.

'A musical isn't *all* dancing, like a ballet,' said Jem. 'It's got acting and singing too. But the dancing in this one is really great.'

It *was*! Lou had to admit it . . . at least to herself. It wasn't formal dancing, like classical ballet, but you could tell that the dancers had been ballet-trained. There was one marvellous scene where the girls argued with the boys about life in America. They sang and danced in a swirl of brilliant colour and movement. Lou loved every minute of it . . . but she wasn't going to say that to Jem. She had to persuade him to do real ballet: she needed him to be her partner . . .

Lou tried to think of some way to put down the musical. She would say that the dancing was not so graceful, that the costumes were too plain, the scenery too dark. And yet she knew in her heart that this only made it more real and powerful.

There was a sword fight in *Romeo and Juliet* when Romeo killed Juliet's cousin. This had become a fight with knives between teenage boys, and when Tony killed Maria's brother, it was so painful that they could hardly bear to watch. Lou and Emma had cried at the end of *Romeo and Juliet*. Now, as *West Side Story* came to its tragic end, they wept buckets, and Orly joined them, handing out tissues from a big box she had ready.

Angela did not cry at all. She gave Jem a superior smile, as if the two of them were the only ones with any sense.

'So? . . . What do you think?' asked
Jem, when it was all over. He looked at
Lou hopefully and she felt really mean as
she prepared to lie.

But while she was wiping her eyes and
blowing her nose, Angela spoke up: 'You
can't possibly compare that to classical
ballet,' she said scornfully. 'I mean, who
wants to watch a gang of boys and a lot

of common girls . . . all living in that horrible city!'

There was a long moment of silence. Lou was speechless with rage. Angela really was the most awful snob in the world! Then, without stopping to think, she said, 'Well, I thought it was brilliant! The music was great and the dancing was amazing! And they weren't common, they were *real*, and that's why it made me cry!'

Suddenly she caught sight of Jem's face and saw that he was grinning.

Oh no! she thought. I went and told the truth.

'I knew you'd like it,' said Jem, 'but I didn't think you'd admit it.'

'Well, I wasn't planning to,' said Lou with a shrug, and they both laughed.

'Now do you see why I want to go to stage school?' said Jem.

'Well, yes,' said Lou reluctantly. She thought hard. 'When will you be going?' she asked.

'Not until he's about sixteen,' said Orly. 'We want him to do his school exams first.'

'Oh well!' said Lou. 'That's all right then!' She felt much better. She had years and years to make him change his mind.

Chapter Seven

It was Friday night and Lou was up in Emma's room. Emma's bed was really cunning, with an extra bed that pulled out from underneath. Whenever she could, Lou liked to come upstairs, lugging her quilt and her pillow, and stay the night.

Now it was late and she and Emma lay in the moonlight making up a story about the adventures of two ballerinas.

Lou loved Emma's room, especially in the moonlight. Her own tiny room at the front of the basement was lit by a streetlamp outside and the sound of passing traffic was never far away. But Emma's room overlooked the quiet of the big back garden and the moon threw a pattern of leaves across her wall. You could pretend you were far away . . . somewhere magical . . . that if you got up and looked out of the window, you would see trees, and wild cliffs and the sea gleaming far below.

The two ballerinas (who were really Lou and Emma grown up) were called Anastasia and Valentina. They had just been offered starring roles in *Swan Lake*: one was to play Odette, the swan princess, and the other Odile, the wicked enchanter's daughter. Suddenly, their adventures were interrupted by raised voices from below.

'Oh no!' said Emma. 'It's Granny Browne. She must be picking on Dad again!'

'Your mum will soon stop her,' said Lou, eager to get on with the story.

'No . . . She's gone to her line-dancing class.'

Mrs Browne had decided to take dancing lessons too and had joined the class at a local hall. Lou and Emma were not quite sure what line-dancing was, but pictured them all moving in a graceful line like the swans in *Swan Lake*.

'I wish we could hear what they're saying,' said Emma anxiously. She seemed to have lost interest in Anastasia and Valentina.

'We could sit on the stairs,' said Lou.

'Do you think we should?' Emma sounded doubtful. 'I mean, I know we

shouldn't really, but I get so worried in
case we have to move away . . . and if I
ask they just say, "Don't worry," or, "It'll
work out." They never give you a straight
"Yes" or "No" . . .'

'Well, if grown-ups don't tell you
anything, they can't complain when you
listen at doors,' said Lou sensibly, and
they tiptoed down the stairs.

*

'I'm sorry, Mother, but my mind is made up.' Mr Browne's voice was firm.

'When I think of the sacrifices I made!' Granny Browne's whiny voice grated on their ears.

Lou squeezed Emma's hand.

Mr Browne said nothing.

'What am I to tell my friends at the bridge club? . . . That my son is a carpenter?'

'Why not?' said Mr Browne. 'It's nothing to be ashamed of.'

'You'll have to sell this house! You may have a golden handshake but the money won't last for ever!'

'We'll manage,' said Mr Browne. 'Val is going back to work and that will help while I'm getting started.'

'Back to *hairdressing*!' Granny Browne sounded outraged.

'She's very good at it,' said Mr Browne. 'And she has time to spare now the children are older.'

Granny Browne snorted. 'I knew you'd go downhill when you married a hairdresser,' she said bitterly. 'You could have married that Patricia – a girl with money, from a good family – but you had to choose a girl from a council estate!'

'I wasn't in love with Patricia,' said Mr Browne patiently. 'I was in love with Val and I still –'

'Oh, *love*!' interrupted Granny Browne. 'That's all young people think about. They're so selfish!'

'Mother,' said Mr Browne, 'I've spent forty years trying to please you and never succeeded. The only time I went against your wishes was when I married Val, and it was the best thing I ever did! She gave me Martin and Emma and everything that matters to me. Val says that if I want to be a carpenter, it's fine with her. And if she wants to be a hairdresser, that's fine with me.' He raised his voice. 'And if you don't like it, Mother, you can go right back to Worthing!'

Lou and Emma cheered silently, waving their fists above their heads.

'I shall go tomorrow,' shrieked Granny Browne. 'I shan't stay here to be insulted by my own son!'

'And now,' said Mr Browne firmly, 'I am going out to my shed.'

The girls shot upstairs as the living-room door opened.

'At this time of night!' screeched Granny Browne.

'Well, it's the only place I can get any peace!'

*

Back in bed, Lou and Emma marvelled.

'It's *so romantic!*' said Lou. 'All that about loving your mum and marrying her when his family didn't approve . . . I mean, it's like *Romeo and Juliet!*'

'Only with a happy ending,' said Emma dreamily.

They lay in the moonlight and tried to imagine Mr and Mrs Browne being young . . . and in love . . . and dancing a lot.

From the bedroom next door came the angry sound of drawers slamming as Granny Browne packed her suitcases. It was like music to their ears.

'What's a golden handshake?' asked Emma.

'Dunno,' said Lou. 'Maybe like that king . . . you know, everything he touched turned to gold.'

'Can't be that,' said Emma. 'Not if my dad's got one.'

'Must be something to do with money . . . We could ask my mum . . .'

'Good idea,' said Emma sleepily.

Lou opened the window to let in the summer night. From the shed at the end of the garden came the faint, sweet sound of music.

Chapter Eight

'It's weird, isn't it?' said Lou to Jem.
'I mean, to think about parents being
young and having rows with their
parents.' She had been telling him about
Mr and Mrs Browne.

'Yes,' said Jem. 'My grandad's family
weren't too happy when he married my
gran.'

They were walking together from
school to ballet class, Jem pushing his
bike along the edge of the kerb.

'But Orly is beautiful,' said Lou, 'and really nice! Why wouldn't they . . .'

'Because she's West Indian,' said Jem. 'I mean, they love her now, but they weren't too pleased at the time.'

They thought about it as they walked on. Lou made a mental note to ask Grandad and Grandma Lambert about their young days, next time she was down in Cornwall.

Then Jem said, 'Are you going to this Summer School thing?'

'I don't think so,' said Lou. 'Are you?'

'Well, yes . . . It's a chance to try all sorts of dance from different countries.'

The notice about the Summer School had appeared on the board at the Maple School the week before. It was being held at a boarding school for dancers while their students were on holiday. Lou wanted to go, but she knew that her mother would not be able to afford it.

'Well, I know I want to do ballet,' she said, 'so I don't need to try other sorts of dance.'

He looked disappointed. 'I thought it would be fun if we all went,' he said. 'Em wants to go if her dad can still afford it, but she says she won't go unless you do.'

It was a problem, thought Lou, but she didn't want to tell him the truth.

'Emma and I don't have to do *everything* together,' she said.

When they reached the Maple School, Jem pushed his bike round the back, out of sight, while Lou headed for the changing room. Emma was nowhere to be seen. This was odd, because Angela and the others from Emma's school were there and one of the mothers usually brought them all by car.

Lou got on with changing and doing her own hair. It was tricky and she was just trying to poke in the stray ends when Emma arrived, very pink and out of breath.

'What happened to you?' asked Lou.

'Don't *ask*!' said Emma. 'I'll tell you later. Just give me a hand with my hair.'

The changing room was already emptying, so it was a bit of a rush. Lou was dying of curiosity: she could feel that something really important had happened. Emma might be pink, but her eyes were bright . . . and although she was late, she didn't seem to be panicking.

When they reached the studio the others were all in position, and their lateness earned them a frown from Mrs Dennison.

It was the last lesson before their grade exams and they worked hard, going through the set exercises several times. They were all doing their very best and Lou could now feel a smoothness and rightness in all her movements that filled her with joy. She tried hard not to let her mind wander, but she couldn't help noticing that Emma seemed very pleased with herself. Not once did Mrs Dennison have to remind her to raise her chin or stand tall.

When the class was over, Mrs Dennison complimented them all. She praised Lou for keeping her mind on her work and Jem for being more disciplined. She told Angela that she must remember to smile more at her audience (Angela scowled).

But Mrs Dennison saved her highest praise for Emma. 'At last,' she said, 'you are growing more confident and this shows in your stance and your gestures. Very well done, Emma!'

Emma gave her a shy but brilliant smile.

'So, what's happened?' hissed Lou as they went back to the changing room. She thought that perhaps there was good news about Emma's dad.

'Not now!' said Emma 'I'll tell you when *they've* gone.'

It was not until the three of them were peacefully ambling home together that Emma told her story . . . and it was not what Lou had expected.

Heaving a big sigh of pleasure and grinning like a Cheshire Cat, Emma said, '*I've* had a *big row* with *Angela!*'

Lou could hardly believe her ears: Emma, who hated even to hear other people quarrelling?

'*You* . . . had a *row* with *Angela?*' she repeated.

'Wow!' said Jem. 'Tell us! Tell us!'

'Well,' began Emma slowly, and then it all came out in a rush. 'There's this new girl at school and she's . . . well, she's actually a bit fat. And Angela was going

71

around saying that it was disgusting and she must be a real pig. But I thought she seemed quite nice. And then Angela said we must all ignore her and keep saying things about her being greedy so that she would overhear . . . and, well, I said I wouldn't do it!'

'Good for you!' said Jem.

'What did she say then?' asked Lou.

'Well, she seemed a bit taken aback.

She started saying it was for the girl's own good . . . because it wasn't healthy to be fat. But I said I thought it was rotten to be mean to someone just because they were different. So then she got cross and said if I didn't go along with it, she wouldn't be friends with me any more. And I said she was a *mean bully* and I didn't *want* to be her friend. Then some of the others started to agree with me, so Angela went all sulky and walked away. Some of her friends went after her, but a lot of the others stayed with me!'

'Oh, Em!' said Lou. 'You are brilliant! You didn't just stand up to her, you actually put her down!'

'Well, yes,' said Emma. 'I suppose I did.' She sounded as if she didn't quite believe it herself.

*

When they were at home and she was alone with Lou, Emma said, 'It was really because of my dad, Lou . . . I mean, him telling Granny Browne how he loved my mum . . . and Martin . . . and me. He made me feel I was really special and I thought, If he can stand up to Granny Browne, I can stand up to Angela! . . . and so I did.'

She smiled at Lou, and Lou grinned back at her.

'Emma Browne,' she said, 'you are amazing!'

Chapter Nine

'Are my knickers
showing?' asked Lou
anxiously.

Her mother
looked. 'No,' she
said. 'You're fine.'

'There's a hairpin
sticking in my
head!'

'Let me see . . .'
Jenny fiddled around

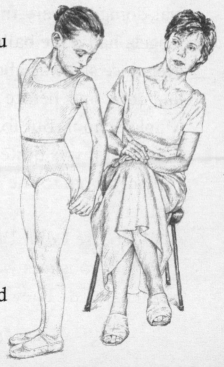

with the bun net. 'How's that?' she asked patiently.

'Better,' said Lou. 'Oh, I do wish I could have gone in with Emma!'

'Mrs Dennison has to match you evenly, you know that. You and Jem and Angela are the best, so she's put you together.'

That was the real trouble, thought Lou. She didn't want Angela around while she was doing her very first grade exam. Angela had done ballet exams before . . . ever since she was about five. Even Jem had done one, before he came to the Maple School. But for Lou it was the first time, and it was quite *terrifying*.

'Did you go to the loo?' asked her mother.

'Of course I did! I'm not *stupid*.'

Her nervousness was making her really bad-tempered. They were using the junior studio as a waiting room. Lou and Angela sat with their mothers, Jem with his grandmother, until it was their turn to perform.

'I wonder how Emma is getting on?' said Jenny.

Emma was in there now. Lou had expected her to be a perfect jelly, but since her row with Angela, she seemed like a different person. *I'm* the one who's a jelly, she thought miserably. I'll muck it all up because I'm so scared and then Angela and Jem will get better marks than me . . . maybe even Emma will get better marks. Emma was her best friend but the thought that she might do better in the grade exams was terrible! I must be a really mean person, thought Lou, and her confidence ebbed away.

Jem came over. 'You look like a scared

rabbit,' he said cheerfully. 'What's the matter?'

'I can't remember *anything*,' said Lou. 'I'm going to get it *all wrong* . . . I'll look really silly . . . Oh, I wish I was Emma! I mean, her exam is nearly over!'

'Calm down!' said Jem. 'It'll be OK. I felt the same the first time.'

'But the examiner won't know I've never done it before,' said Lou. 'She'll think I've done it lots of times . . . like Angela.'

'I expect Mrs Dennison's told her,' said Jem. 'I mean, they do get to chat a bit before it starts.'

'Do you think so?' Lou thought about it. 'Angela will tell everyone if I make a mess of it,' she said gloomily.

'You *won't* make a mess of it . . . Come on, Lou, cheer up! You know what Mrs

Dennison said: "Do your best, try to enjoy it and smile at the examiner . . . because she's your audience."'

Lou sighed. Mrs Dennison had once said, 'Lou loves her audience, that is her strong point.' Did that mean that she had to love the examiner? Fat chance! she thought.

The door of the waiting room opened and Emma came in, smiling and glowing, with two of the other girls.

Mrs Dennison appeared and asked, 'How did it go?'

'Oh, it was great!' said Emma. 'I mean, she was really nice. I forgot something in the middle but she just reminded me quietly and then I got it right.' She looked at Lou, who was nearly shaking with fright. 'You'll be fine, Lou,' she said, and gave her a quick hug.

'Come along now.' Mrs Dennison gathered her next three students together and steered them towards the door.

There were little cries of encouragement from the anxious parents and then they were crossing the quiet corridor towards the exam studio.

'Break a leg!' hissed Jem, and they went through the door . . .

An hour later, they sat in the Cosy Corner, laughing and talking and stuffing themselves with cream cakes. Jenny Lambert, Orly Sinclair and Val Browne smiled at each other above their heads.

'I told you you'd be fine!' said Jem. 'It was Angela who went wrong.'

'She covered it up pretty quickly,' said Lou.

'That was clever,' said Jem, 'but the scowl was a mistake!'

'She was nice, wasn't she?' said Emma.

'Who? Angela!'

'No, the examiner. You know what I mean.'

'Just teasing,' said Jem. 'Yes, I thought she'd be a battleaxe but she was quite young and friendly.'

Lou wasn't saying a lot. She had not quite recovered yet. She was just enjoying her meringue, and the lovely feeling of relief that came from knowing that it was all over and that she hadn't made a fool of herself. There would be lots more ballet exams, but it would never be so bad again. She knew what to expect now.

'One down and one to go,' said Jenny, smiling. She had her evening-class exam the next week.

'Don't *worry*,' said Lou confidently. 'You'll be all right!'

'Will you tell me if my knickers are showing,' said her mother, 'and remind me to go to the loo?'

It took a moment for Lou to get the joke, and then they both laughed together.

Chapter Ten

It seemed like a lifetime as they waited for the results to come.

Mrs Dennison said that she felt sure they would all pass and Emma said that was enough for her. But Lou dreamed of being Commended or even Highly Commended. She knew that Jem had been Highly Commended in his earlier exam and she guessed that he was after a Distinction. Only Angela had had a Distinction before . . .

When the day came and the results went up on the Maple School's notice-board, Lou couldn't bear to look. She hung around at the back, while the others crowded forward.

She heard Emma's cry of delight. 'I didn't just pass,' she called, 'I got a Commended!'

'What did I get?' asked Lou.

Emma studied the list and then turned to her with a face that gave nothing away.

'You'd better see for yourself,' she said.

Oh, please let it be Highly Commended, thought Lou, if Emma got Commended. She felt a bit mean wanting to do better than Emma, when Emma was her best friend. Jem turned away from the board; he was grinning like an idiot.

'You got it!' said Lou. 'Didn't you? You got your Distinction!'

'Look for yourself,' said Jem.

Lou could not bring herself to look for her own name. Instead she looked at the column that gave the standard reached. There were two Distinctions in their class: Jem, she thought, and Angela, of course. She glanced across the page. The

name was Jerome Sinclair and the second
. . . Lucy Lambert. For a moment she
couldn't believe it! She searched for
Angela's name and saw Highly
Commended. Lucy couldn't speak. She
turned away from the board and stared at
Emma. She still couldn't quite believe her
eyes.

'I didn't tell you,' said Emma. 'I
thought you ought to see for yourself.'

As the shock faded, happiness flooded
in, and soon everyone was hugging
everyone else. Only Angela didn't seem
too pleased in spite of the congratulations
of her friends.

The Wind-up Merchant was throwing a
party. He said it was because he liked
parties and to celebrate their successes –
Lou's mum had passed her exams too –

and for something else that would be a surprise. It was a wonderful party. There was a big striped tent on his back lawn and a barbecue and people going around with delicious nibbly things on trays. There was even a bouncy castle.

When everyone had eaten, the Wind-up Merchant sent round champagne, and fizzy lemonade for the children. Then he made a speech. He said how well they had all done, including Lou's mum.

'But I have another reason for this party,' he went on. 'This is an important day for me too. I spent many years building up a successful business, which I sold a few years ago when I retired. But I found I got rather bored without it. I did pantomimes and magic shows and all the things I'd always wanted to do. But there was still a lot of time left over. Then I found a new interest. When Lucy told me to see Emma's dad if I needed a new kitchen, I took her advice.

Mr Browne was planning a new business, giving up banking to be a carpenter and fit new kitchens. He wanted to do all the woodwork, rather than the business side, so I suggested we should become partners and he agreed. So this is a party to launch the new firm of Peter Browne and Henry Mumford . . . or Cosy Kitchens as we are calling it for short!' Then he proposed a toast and as they all raised their glasses, a brilliant display of fireworks went off at the far end of the garden.

Lou went to sleep in Emma's room that night but not until very late because they were both too excited. Things had turned

out well for everyone, except perhaps for
Angela and Granny Browne.

'You won't move, will you?' said
Emma. 'I mean now that your mum has
passed her exams.'

'Don't worry,' said Lou. 'We've agreed
that even if we don't have a lot of room,
we like living in your house.'

They lay in a happy silence and then
Emma said, 'There's something else you
don't know yet.'

'What?' said Lou. 'Tell me!'

'I'm coming to your school next year.'

Lou sat up in bed to stare at her.

'Really?' she said. 'Oh, wow! Is it because of the fees?'

'No,' said Emma. 'They could afford the fees because of Mr Mumford being a partner in the business. But I put my foot down. I told my mum and dad that they were both doing what *they* wanted to do, and what *I* wanted was to go to school with you and Jem. And my mum said, "Let her, Peter. It's a good school and I went to my local school when I was her age." And my dad kissed her and said if local schools could turn out girls like my mum, then that's where I should go!'

'Oh, great!' said Lou. 'I can't wait. It'll be brilliant!'

But she also had her secret. 'There's

something you don't know too,' she said.

'What? Tell me!' said Emma.

'Well, when I phoned my grandad and grandma in Cornwall, to tell them about my Distinction, Grandad was so pleased he said they would pay for me to go to the Summer School . . . if I promise to teach him all the foreign dances next time I'm down there.'

'Oh, Lou, that's brilliant,' said Emma. 'Have you told Jem?'

'I'll tell him tomorrow. I wanted to tell you first.'

'Now we'll all be together,' said Emma. 'Oh, Lou, won't it be great!'

'Fantastic!' said Lou. 'So now we can get back to Anastasia and Valentina . . .'

Dancing Shoes

Hi!

After all that worrying, everything has worked out brilliantly. Em's coming to my school next year and, even better, Granny Browne has gone! I can't believe I got a Distinction in my ballet exam – I was so nervous.

I can't wait to start the Summer Dance course with Emma and Jem. It's going to be great – all of us together for a whole week, learning about different types of dance from all over the world. I'm sure I won't like them better than ballet though. Now all I have to do is make sure that Jem feels the same way, otherwise he'll never be my partner when I'm a famous ballerina!

Love

Lou

PS You can join me, Emma and Jem (and even horrible Angela!) at Summer School in DANCING SHOES: LUCY'S NEXT STEP. Don't miss it!